NO DRAGONS for TEA

Fire Safety for Kids
(and DRAGONS)

Written by Jean Pendziwol
Illustrated by Martine Gourbault

Kids Can Press

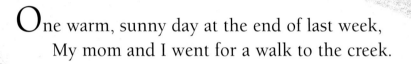

One warm, sunny day at the end of last week,
My mom and I went for a walk to the creek.

As I raced down the hill
in my little red wagon,

I veered to the left and smacked into a dragon.

I suppose he could see there was fear in my eyes,
As I jumped to my feet, quite filled with surprise.

He sheepishly grinned and stepped out of the way,
But he seemed so polite that I asked him to play.

He had a cute bear and some other toys too;
With my shovel and pail, we'd have oodles to do.

We ran to the creek and then on to the bay,
Where we played on the beach for the rest of the day.

Then Mom waved and said, "Now it's time to go eat,
Let's pack the red wagon and head up the street."

It's hard to stop playing with friends old or new,
So I asked if the dragon could come to eat, too.

Mom wrinkled her brow and squinted her eyes,
Looking up at the dragon's incredible size.

I begged and I pleaded, then said, very sweet,
"We won't make a mess; we'll be tidy and neat!"

So at last she said, "Yes. Just this once I'll agree,
You may have the dragon come over for tea."

We had carrots and apples, thick slices of ham,
With fresh homemade biscuits and strawberry jam,

Cold glasses of milk and a great big dill pickle,
But the pepper we sprinkled sure made my nose tickle!

Then the dragon's nose twitched, and he started to wheeze.
His eyes misted up, and he blew a great sneeze.

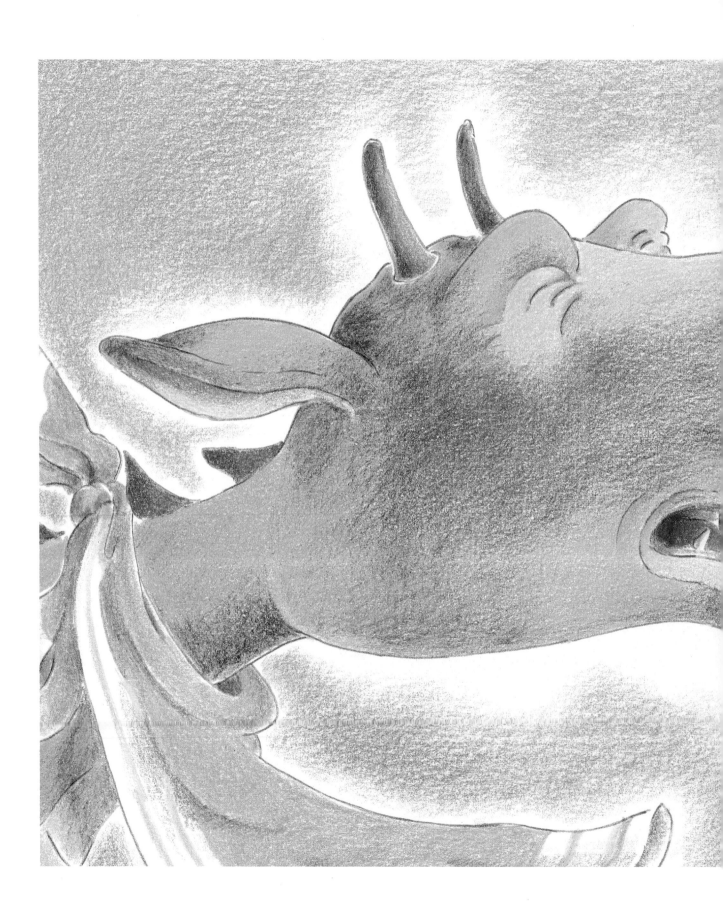

A-A-A-CHOOOOOO!

Well ... we all know what happens when dragons "a-choo."
Flames shot from his mouth and from both nostrils too.

Our tablecloth sparked and then burst into flame,
And the curtains that hung right beside did the same!

The smoke alarm rang. What a loud, piercing sound!
It meant "Get out fast!" so I dropped to the ground.

The room filled with smoke as I crawled on the floor
And started to make my way to the front door.

The dragon got scared and decided to hide,
But I knew when there's fire, we must get outside.

I grabbed his thick tail and with one mighty tug,
I pulled that big dragon from under the rug.

A-A-A-CHOOOOOO!

Well … we all know what happens when dragons "a-choo."
Flames shot from his mouth and from both nostrils too.

I crept down the hallway and said, "Follow me,
I know the way out — we must meet by the tree."

So Mom and the dragon and I all met there,

Then that silly old dragon went back for his bear!

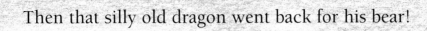

We ran up and caught him and wouldn't let go,
And I said, "Listen, Dragon, here's what you should know:

"Don't ever go back — that just will not do.
We can get a new bear, but we can't replace you."

Since the fire was burning inside of our home,
We went to the neighbor's to borrow the phone.

Mom knew what to dial and said, calm and clear,
"Here's our full street address — send the fire trucks here."

Before very long, down our street they came sailing,
With bright red lights flashing and loud sirens wailing.

The fire crew rushed to start work on their tasks.
They were dressed in big boots and wore helmets and masks.

They hooked up the hose and ran into the house,
Where they sprayed streams of water in order to douse

The table, the curtains, our lovely snack too,
And it didn't take long till that fire was through.

The fire chief called out the door with a shout,
"The smoke made a mess, but the fire is out!"

My poor friend the dragon knew he was to blame,
So he hung down his head and wept great tears of shame.

One of the fire crew said, "Don't be sad,
You knew what to do, and of that we're quite glad.

"You all got out safely — that's really what matters."
Then she took us to see the big pump truck and ladders.

The dragon put on a shiny red hat,
And I asked to see where the fire crew sat.

She showed us the siren, the hoses and lights,
And the ladders they climb up to reach higher heights.

The rest of the fire crew checked all the rooms,
While a fan in the door blew out gray smoke and fumes.

Then the dragon and I, we sat down for a while.
I reached up and hugged him. He gave me a smile.

The next time the dragon and I want to play,
We'll pack up a picnic and go to the bay.

We are friends, tried and true, the best we can be,
But I'll never again invite dragons for tea!

The Dragon's Fire-Safety Rhyme

When the smoke alarm sounds, here's what you should do:
Leave your toys all behind, 'cause there's only one you.

Get down and stay low, crawling under the smoke,
Because breathing those fumes in might make you choke.

If your clothes catch on fire, don't run about,
"Stop, drop and roll" till the flames are all out.

Don't open a door if the handle feels hot.
Find another way out to your planned meeting spot.

Even when scared, you must never hide,
And once you are out, don't go back inside!

The dragon now knows what to do in a fire. Do the children in your care? Fire safety does not need to be a frightening topic. *No Dragons for Tea* provides an ideal opportunity to teach children about fire safety in a non-threatening way. Children will pick up lots of safety tips as they follow the dragon and little girl through the story. But it is also important for children to know what to do in their own home, school or day care.

Here is a checklist to discuss and to put into action together:

- What is the fire-emergency phone number in your area? Learn it and practice saying your name, address and the nearest intersection to your home. Never call from inside a burning building. Get out and use a neighbor's phone or a public telephone.

- Find out where your smoke detectors are and listen to what they sound like. The smoke detectors' batteries should be changed twice a year.

- Make a fire-escape plan and choose a meeting place that everyone agrees on. The spot should be safe to get to, permanent and easy to remember — such as a tree in the yard, the neighbor's front step or a streetlight. When staying someplace different, such as Grandma and Grandpa's or a hotel, take time to make a new escape plan.

- Once outside, you must never go back inside a burning building or one where the smoke alarm or fire detector is ringing. Stay outside until the building has been checked and is safe. Wait at your meeting place so that everyone can be accounted for.

- Practice what to do in different fire-emergency situations. Don't take any toys with you, and don't stop to change your clothes. Feel closed doors before opening them. If they are hot, don't open them. Find another way out, such as a window.

Learn how to remove window screens and unlock windows so that they can be used as exits in an emergency. Remember that the most important thing is to get out of the building.

- Never, ever hide!

- If your clothing catches on fire, never run. Learn and practice "stop, drop and roll." Stretch out on the ground, cover your face with your hands, and roll from side to side to smother the flames.

- Hold a practice drill. The drill does not need to be a surprise: it is meant to help you learn what to do.

- Never play with matches — they are tools, not toys. Learn what other things could be dangerous in your home, school or day care — such as hot stoves, curling irons, coffeepots, electric heaters and fireplaces — and don't touch them.

- Visit your local fire station or ask a fire prevention officer to speak about fire safety to your class or other group. Remember that firefighters are safe strangers, even though they can look scary when they are wearing their full fire-fighting gear.

- Learn the dragon's fire-safety rhyme and be fire safe!